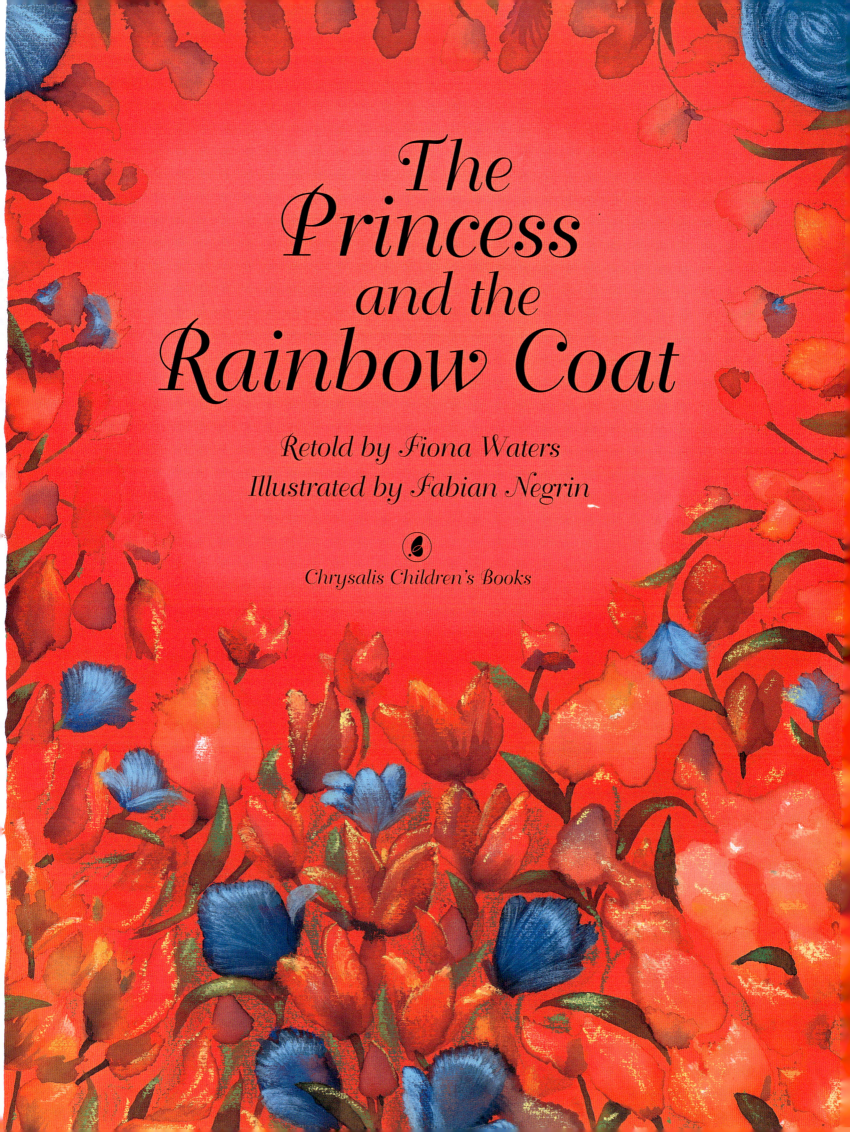

The Princess and the Rainbow Coat

Retold by Fiona Waters

Illustrated by Fabian Negrin

Chrysalis Children's Books

For Kendra, with much love from GAF – FW

To Ruy and Simona – FN

First published in Great Britain in 2005
by Chrysalis Children's Books
an imprint of Chrysalis Books Group Plc
The Chrysalis Building, Bramley Road, London W10 6SP
www.chrysalisbooks.co.uk

Retelling copyright © Fiona Waters 2005
Illustrations copyright © Fabian Negrin 2005

The moral right of the author and illustrator has been asserted.

Designed by Sarah Goodwin.

A CIP catalogue record for this book is available
from the British Library.

ISBN 1 84365 024 X

Set in Cochin
Printed in China

2 4 6 8 10 9 7 5 3 1

This book can be ordered direct from the publisher. Please contact
the Marketing Department. But try your bookshop first.

A time there was when a noble king ruled his tiny kingdom with wisdom and kindness. His queen was as gentle as he was wise, and as beautiful as he was kind. She had golden hair that tumbled down her back and no one in the kingdom was as lovely except her own little daughter, Elianor.

Elianor was very much loved by her parents, and indeed the whole court, for she possessed a sweet nature and had a love of small creatures. Bright-eyed little birds would eat cake crumbs from her fingers, and bushy-tailed squirrels would seek out the nuts that she always kept in her pocket. She grew up surrounded by beauty for both the king and the queen loved collecting and the palace was filled with rich and precious objects. Water clocks of the finest jade from China, heavy leather-bound books of herb lore, sparkling crystal goblets from Bohemia and mysteriously curled seashells all had their own special place along the walls of the sunlit corridors. And in the garden bloomed rare and exotic flowers. Delicate green orchids sheltered under the boughs of the tamarisk trees, huge white tree peonies hung over the paths and the air was heavy with the scent of the rich creamy frangipani flowers and clouds of purple lavender.

But then the sly hand of fate dealt Elianor a terrible blow. Within days of each other, both her parents died, and she was left to fend for herself. As is sometimes the case, the wise old councillors of the kingdom could not see beyond their own noses, and their first and only concern became the safekeeping of the kingdom. Elianor must be married as soon as ever possible, and, without pausing to consider Elianor's own feelings in the matter, they arranged for her to marry a prince from a kingdom across the seas. When he arrived with his retinue, Elianor was horrified to find that not only was Prince Norris as old as the hills and ugly to boot, but he was loud and uncouth. He trampled all over the orchids as he stamped through the gardens, he terrified the little birds with his huge voice and he swept fragile treasures off the shelves as he barged through the palace.

Elianor decided to take matters into her own hands. She summoned the councillors to the throne room. "If I am to be married, I must have suitable clothes in my trousseau. My mother would have insisted on it. You must have three dresses made for me. The first shall be as golden yellow as the sun. The second must shimmer silver like the moon, and the third must glitter and twinkle like the midnight stars. They must be spun from the finest silkworms and be so fine that each will fit into a walnut shell."

The councillors were muttering amongst themselves. Whatever would such finery cost?

But Elianor had not finished. "You must also make me a coat, a rainbow coat of feathers from all the birds of the air, and not one single sparrow must be hurt in the weaving of this coat." She turned on her heel, ignoring the anxious councillors and the sulky Prince Norris, and walked slowly out of the throne room, head held high. That should put paid to all that nonsense, the tasks were quite impossible, she thought.

But she was wrong. Within a horribly short space of time, the three dresses were presented to Elianor. The first was as golden yellow as the sun. The second shimmered silver like the moon, and the third glittered and twinkled like the midnight stars.

They were so fine that each fitted into a walnut shell. And the coat, the rainbow coat of feathers from all the birds of the air, lay glowing across the crimson draped bed.

"And by the way, the wedding is arranged for tomorrow, Princess Elianor," smirked the councillors as they bowed their way out of the bedroom.

Elianor sank to her knees, her face buried in the beautiful rainbow coat. And as she stroked the soft feathers, she realized that she too must fly. She must run away, and that very night, if she was to avoid her marriage the next day to Prince Norris.

She waited until every one of the myriad clocks in the palace had finished chiming midnight, and then she brushed her golden hair and tied it all up into a black scarf. She took off her golden rings and bracelets, her fine embroidered dress and her satin slippers, and put on a plain cotton shift and a pair of heavy wooden clogs. Then she put on the rainbow coat. She placed the three dresses very carefully inside the walnut shells and hid them deep in a pocket of the coat. Then she tiptoed out of her bedroom, down the long corridors, past the empty throne room and out through the palace gates. She slipped, soft as a shadow, through the garden and crossed the wooden bridge over the fast flowing river outside the palace walls, and entered the forest silently. No one saw her go, and not a beast stirred as she passed.

Elianor walked all night and all the next day and all the following night too, so anxious was she to put as much distance as possible between herself and the dreadful Prince Norris. But by the third night, she could barely keep her eyes open and so she curled up, pillowed warmly in the rainbow coat, in a hollow tree and there she fell into a dreamless sleep.

Dawn broke, and, as the forest birds began to wake, they discovered Elianor, still fast asleep. They fluttered around but not one wanted to wake the sleeping princess, for somehow they knew that she needed their protection. The sun rose, and still Elianor slept. The birds circled the hollow tree, calling softly to each other, as the forest slowly came to life. A passing fox paused in astonishment at the rainbow-coloured bird, but he passed on by silently. The secretive badger paused in his bustle home at the sight of such a rare creature, but he hated company so he too hurried off. And then in the distance came the bray of a hunting horn. A tumult of barking rose and a pack of hounds came wagging and sniffing up to the hollow tree. The king who owned the forest was out with his hawks and a great troop of courtiers and huntsmen.

"There must be some animal in that tree," said the king to the huntsmen. "Go and see what it is."

They came back in great excitement. "Your Majesty, it is a strange creature, all covered in feathers of every imaginable hue, and it is fast asleep," they cried.

"Try to catch it alive and bring it to me. We shall take it back to the palace," ordered the king.

Well, of course, as soon as the huntsmen laid hands on Elianor, she awoke and was quite terrified by the sight of so many people. She didn't want them to know who she was in case word of her flight from Prince Norris had reached the king, so she pretended she was unable to speak. But the king, who was astonished to find the strange creature was in fact a young girl, saw how frightened she was and so he ordered the huntsmen to treat her with consideration and take her back to the palace.

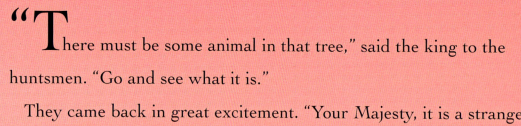

Once there, the king tried to find out who she was but Elianor would speak not a word. He had a room made ready for her in the palace, and insisted she be allowed to have a bath and some breakfast. He was puzzled by Elianor's obvious air of elegance and the fabulous rainbow coat, yet she wore clumsy clogs and a simple shift. Here was a mystery he could not fathom.

But still Elianor kept silent and so the king sent her to work in the palace kitchens. The cook, who could barely boil an egg, was pleased to have a skivvy to do all the hard work and so poor Elianor was kept busy from morn to night, peeling vegetables, plucking the chickens, gutting the fish and washing dishes. And so, many months passed. Elianor was happy to have escaped the awful Prince Norris, but she did not wish to spend the rest of her life in a hot, steamy kitchen being shouted at by the crabby and lazy cook. Every night when she fell exhausted into bed, she would take out the three walnut shells and look at them sadly.

Then one day came the exciting news that the king was to give a great masked ball. Of course, the cook was thrown into a great temper and she shouted at Elianor even more than usual for, as you might imagine, the preparations were considerable. Elianor had barely a moment to breathe in the days before the great occasion, but when the last towering blancmange and the last dish of iced fruits had been sent up to the banqueting hall on the night of the ball, Elianor slipped quietly to her room. She washed all the grease and smells of the kitchen away and, very carefully, cracked open the first walnut and took out the dress as golden yellow as the sun, and slipped it over her head. She brushed her golden hair and covered her face with a simple golden mask and then, trembling with excitement, she followed the sound of the music to the ballroom.

The moment she entered, there was a gasp of wonder. No one had ever seen such a beauty. Who was she, and where did she come from? No one knew. There was a babble of talk. Handsome young men queued up by her side and eventually even the king himself asked her to dance. As soon as the dance was over, Elianor sank into a deep curtsey, and the king bowed very low but when he looked up, the beautiful stranger had vanished! No one had seen where she went. The guards at the palace gates were questioned, and then shouted at, but they were insistent that no one had come in or out. Slowly the musicians took up their instruments again, and the dancing began once more. Elianor, meanwhile, had taken off her dress as golden yellow as the sun and was back in the kitchen looking in some dismay at the huge pile of dirty dishes.

The next day, and for weeks after, all the palace talk was of the mysterious girl. It was whispered that she had quite bewitched the king, and certainly he was not his usual cheerful self. Within a very short time, he announced that there would be another ball. He gave the guards very special instructions to look out for the beautiful stranger.

Once again, Elianor was rushing hither and thither in the kitchen at the behest of the cook, but on the night of the ball, as soon as the last rich meringue and the last great bowl of raspberries had been sent up to the banqueting hall, she slipped quietly to her room. She washed all the grease and smells of the kitchen away and, very carefully, cracked open the second walnut and took out the dress that shimmered silver like the moon, and slipped it over her head. She brushed her golden hair and covered her face with a simple silver mask, and made her way to the ballroom.

Once again, the moment she entered, everyone turned to look at this beautiful girl who had suddenly appeared as if from nowhere. The king wasted no time in claiming her for his own, and he danced with her time and time again before offering her a glass of champagne. But when he turned to give her the sparkling glass, she had vanished as if she had never been. Everyone started talking at once. The king was heartbroken. The guards were dismayed. Elianor, meanwhile, had taken off her dress that shimmered silver like the moon, and was back in the kitchen looking yet again at a huge pile of dirty dishes.

The king was determined to find out who the beautiful stranger was, but no one, absolutely no one, could tell him anything at all that might lead to her. There was nothing for it. He would have to give another ball. The cook was livid. Elianor just smiled as she went about the enormous preparations. On the night, as soon as the last chocolate trifle and the last gilded pineapple had been sent up to the banqueting hall, she slipped quietly to her room. She washed all the grease and smells of the kitchen away and, very carefully, cracked open the third walnut and took out the dress that glittered and twinkled like the midnight stars, and slipped it over her head. She brushed her golden hair and covered her face with a simple sparkling mask, and made her way to the ballroom.

The king had been pacing the ballroom floor, up and down, but as soon as he saw his mysterious lady, he ran to her side and clasped her hand very tightly in his. "Tonight, fair lady, you shall not escape me!" he cried and his joy was plain to see. And they danced, and sipped champagne, and danced some more, and never once did the king let go of Elianor's hand. And then, perhaps it was the bubbles from the champagne, but the king sneezed and in that moment he dropped Elianor's hand. She whirled round and out of the room, down the long corridors towards her room. But everyone was in fast pursuit and she only had time to cover the dress that glittered and twinkled like the midnight stars with her rainbow coat before she dashed into the kitchen and began pouring water over the great pile of dirty dishes. The king and all the courtiers piled into the kitchen just behind her, breathing heavily.

"Where is she?" demanded the frantic king. "You must have seen her, the beautiful stranger, she most assuredly came this way," he said to Elianor's back, but she just went on quietly stacking the dishes. Then as she moved, the rainbow coat fell open and there for all to see was the dress that glittered and twinkled like midnight stars.

"It has been you all this time!" the king exclaimed in astonishment as he led Elianor firmly away from the dirty dishes, and up into his private rooms so he could talk to her without the entire court (and the absolutely terrified cook) looking on.

Elianor told him the whole story. She told him of her beloved parents and the palace filled with rich and precious objects. She told him about the old councillors of the kingdom who could not see beyond their own noses, and she told him about the ghastly Prince Norris who was as old as the hills and ugly to boot. The king looked into her eyes and, still holding her hand very firmly, told her he wished very much that she might marry him instead of Prince Norris. And Elianor, still holding his hand very firmly, said she would very much like to marry him.

And so the next day they were married, and they had another ball to celebrate their marriage. But this time, the cook had to do all the work herself!